Contents

Ladybird books are widely available, but in case of
difficulty may be ordered by post or telephone from:

Ladybird Books – Cash Sales Department
Littlegate Road Paignton Devon TQ3 3BE
Telephone 01803 554761

A catalogue record for this book is available
from the British Library

Published by Ladybird Books Ltd Loughborough Leicestershire UK
Ladybird Books Inc Auburn Maine 04210 USA

Storytime
for
2
year olds

by JOAN STIMSON

illustrated by
JOHN and CAROLINE ASTROP

Ladybird

I'd like to…

I'd like to be a doctor,
I'd like to fly a plane,
I'd like to cut your hair,
I'd like to drive a crane.

I'd like to be a farmer,
I'd like to be a cook,
But just before I start…
I'd like to read this book.

Christine's cornflakes

Christine was a very greedy hippo. But she only liked one thing… cornflakes.

One morning Mum made a dreadful discovery. There were no more cornflakes in the cupboard.

'I WANT MY CORNFLAKES,' yelled Christine. She banged her spoon on the table.

Mum sent William to the shop. 'Here's enough money for TEN packets of cornflakes. You can take Dad's wheelbarrow.'

The other hippos got on with their breakfast.

'Try some of my toast,' said Toby.

'Don't want any,' said Christine. But then her tummy rumbled. So she tried a small nibble of toast, then a bigger nibble.

'Try some of my apple,' said Albert.

'Don't want any,' said Christine. But then her tummy rumbled. So she tried a small bite of apple, then a bigger bite.

'Try some of my porridge,' said Polly.

'Don't want any,' said Christine. But then her tummy rumbled. So she tried a small spoonful. AND THEN CHRISTINE SPOONED UP THE LOT!

'CORNFLAKES!' called William. He wheeled Dad's barrow into the kitchen.

'Don't want any,' said Christine. She gave a little burp. 'I'm TOO FULL... for cornflakes!'

Wally Wally Whale

Wally Wally Whale
Had a ten foot tail –
He chased all the fishes
When he went for a sail.

Molly Molly Whale
Had a TWENTY foot tail –
She CAUGHT all the fishes
When *she* went for a sail.

I want to fly a dragon

I want to fly a dragon
Right across the sky.
I want to fly a dragon
(Or be a dragonfly)!

The
dirty
dinosaur

'Just look at your knees, Douglas!' cried Mrs Dinosaur.

'Brrrm, brrrm,' said Douglas. He was MUCH too busy with his car to look at his knees.

'Have you seen your face, Douglas?' asked Mr Dinosaur.

'Brrrm, brrrm,' said Douglas. He was MUCH too busy driving his car to look in the mirror.

'Don't you EVER take a bath?' sighed Granny Dinosaur.

'Brrrm, brrrm,' said Douglas. He NEVER had time for a bath.

One day the dinosaurs went to town. On their way they passed a sign. 'CAR WASH,' it said, in big letters.

13

'Brrrm, brrrm,' said Douglas. He couldn't wait to get inside. 'Ooooh!' he cried. 'It tickles… but I like it!'

'Come out of there, Douglas,' cried Mum, Dad and Granny Dinosaur.

At last Douglas came out of the car wash. 'That was lovely!' he cried. And for the first time ever, Douglas was clean… ALL OVER.

Stop,
look,
listen!

'STOP, LOOK, LISTEN,' said
Mrs Snail firmly. She was teaching
Dennis and Doreen to cross the path.

'I'm hungry,' cried Dennis. 'And I can
see some leaves on the other side of the
path.'

'STOP, LOOK, LISTEN,' said
Mrs Snail. She held him back.

'DING-A-LING-LING!'

'Look out!' cried Dennis. 'It's a big boy on a bike.'

Mrs Snail waited patiently. The children grumbled. The boy rode up and down the path on his bike.

'I'm starving,' wailed Doreen. 'And I can see my lunch.'

'STOP, LOOK, LISTEN,' said Mrs Snail.

'RUMBLE, RUMBLE, RUMBLE!'

'LOOK OUT!' cried Doreen. 'It's a great big girl with a pram.'

Mrs Snail waited patiently. The children grumbled. The girl pushed her doll up and down the path.

'We want lunch, we want lunch,' chanted Dennis and Doreen.

'STOP, LOOK, LISTEN,' said
Mrs Snail.

'LUNCHTIME!' called a huge lady
from the house. But she wasn't calling
the snails!

Dennis and Doreen burst into tears.
The boy got off his bike. The girl left her
pram. And they ran inside together.

'STOP, LOOK, LISTEN,' said
Mrs Snail kindly.

'I can't SEE anything,' said Dennis.

'I can't HEAR anything,' said Doreen.

'NOW it's safe,' said Mrs Snail.

And they all crossed the path.

20

Red

Red is the ladybird having fun,
Red is the poppy asleep in the sun,
Red are the cherries down in the shop,
Red is the light that tells us STOP!

Green

Green is the frog, who croaks so late,
Green are the peas piled high on
  my plate.
Green is the grass my Dad has to mow,
Green is the light that tells us GO!

Turkeys

The turkeys are making
A terrible fuss.
They're bored with waiting
To get on the bus.

They're flapping and fighting –
Oh, what a to do!
If only those turkeys
Could learn how to queue.

The race

One day Farmer Brown went to market. While he was away, the farm animals decided to have a race.

Roger Ram jumped onto Farmer Brown's tractor. Bernie Bull jumped onto Mrs Brown's bike. Gary Goat jumped onto Billy Brown's skateboard.

'Hey! What about me?' clucked Hilary Hen. But no one was listening.

'Ready,' cried Roger. 'Steady,' roared Bernie. 'GO!' yelled Gary. And they all rushed off together.

'Hey! Wait for me!' clucked Hilary. She jumped into Jenny Brown's trainers, which were far too big for her.

Roger was soon in front. But not for long.

'POP, SPLUTTER, POP,' went the tractor. It had run out of petrol.

Bernie sped past Roger. But not for long.

'THUMP, THUD, THUMP,' went Mrs Brown's bike. Bernie was too heavy for a bike. He'd squashed the tyres flat.

Gary overtook Roger and Bernie. But not for long.

'*Wheeee*… SPLASH!' went the skateboard. Gary wasn't looking where he was going. He landed in the duckpond.

'Hey!' clucked Hilary. She shuffled past Roger, Bernie and Gary. 'I'M GOING TO WIN!'

And that's just what she did.

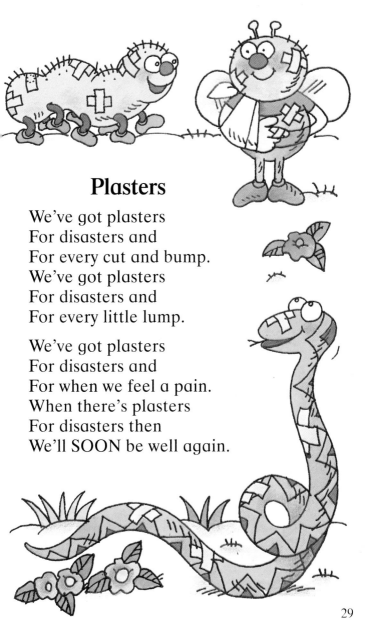

Plasters

We've got plasters
For disasters and
For every cut and bump.
We've got plasters
For disasters and
For every little lump.

We've got plasters
For disasters and
For when we feel a pain.
When there's plasters
For disasters then
We'll SOON be well again.

29

The ice cream van

Run, run, as fast as you can,
I hear the sound of the ice cream van.

Wait, wait, wait in the queue,
I'm very hungry, how about you?

Look, look, look what he's got –
I can't choose… let's eat the lot!

Where's Teddy?

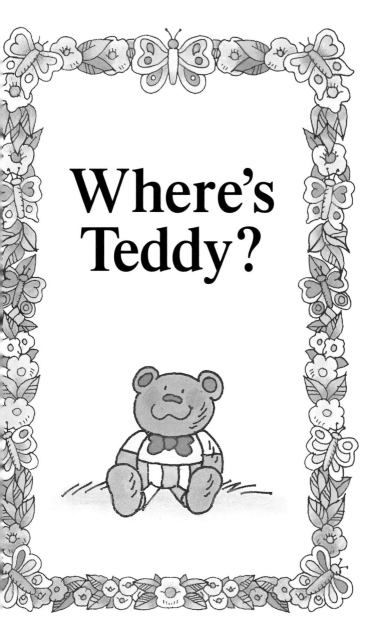

'Where's Teddy?' cried Brian the elephant. He couldn't find him anywhere.

'Have YOU seen Teddy?' Brian asked the monkeys.

'Yes,' said the monkeys. 'He came for a swing in the trees. And we gave him a banana. But he's gone now.'

'Have YOU seen Teddy?' Brian asked the kangaroos.

'Yes,' cried Jumper. 'He came for a ride in my pouch. Up and down he went. But he's gone now.'

'Have YOU seen Teddy?' Brian asked the polar bears.

'Yes,' cried Roly Poly Bear. 'He came for a swim on my back. And splashed all my friends. But he's gone now.'

'Have YOU seen Teddy?' Brian asked the giraffes.

'Yes,' said the giraffes. 'We all had a game of hide and seek. But he's gone now.'

'Have YOU seen Teddy?' Brian asked
the zookeeper.

'Yes,' said Bert. 'He helped to eat up
my tea. But he's gone now.'

Brian trudged home. It was getting late. 'I think I'll put on my pyjamas,' he yawned.

Brian went into the bedroom. And there, tucked up and waiting for him was... TEDDY!

Stop it!

STOP IT! cried the tiger,
I'm ticklish, can't you see?
I'm ticklish on my stripes.
I'm ticklish on my knee.

STOP IT! cried the tiger,
There's something I must do.
It's time for ME to tickle –
For ME to tickle YOU!

Bubbles

I love bubbles in the bath,
I love bubbles in the sink,
But the bubbles I love best
Are the bubbles in my DRINK!

Not
sleepy

'I'M NOT SLEEPY!' yelled Zoe Zebra.

She jumped out of bed and ran downstairs. Mrs Zebra gave her a drink and sent her upstairs again.

'I'M NOT SLEEPY!' cried Zoe. She started to play with her train set.

'Get back into bed,' called Mrs Zebra.

'I'M NOT SLEEPY!' grumbled Zoe. She started to do a jigsaw puzzle.

41

'Put that puzzle away,' called
Mrs Zebra. 'You'll lose all the pieces
down the bed.'

'I'M NOT SLEEPY!' yawned Zoe. She
started to read a book.

'Don't read too late,' called Mrs Zebra.

'I'm not sleepy,' whispered Zoe. She started to count her stripes.

'I'm coming up to tuck you in,' called Mrs Zebra.

'Zzzzz, zzzzz,' snored Zoe.